Ben The Raindrop

Strength in Perseverance

Peter W. Carbone, MBA

AuthorHouse™
1663 Liberty Drive
Bloomington, IN 47403
www.authorhouse.com
Phone: 833-262-8899

Because of the dynamic nature of the Internet, any web addresses or links contained in this book may have changed since publication and may no longer be valid. The views expressed in this work are solely those of the author and do not necessarily reflect the views of the publisher, and the publisher hereby disclaims any responsibility for them.

This book is printed on acid-free paper.

ISBN: 978-1-4343-4339-0 (sc)

Library of Congress Control Number: 2007907717

Print information available on the last page.

Published by AuthorHouse 03/02/2021

Peter W. Carbone, MBA

Copyright © 2005

authorHOUSE®

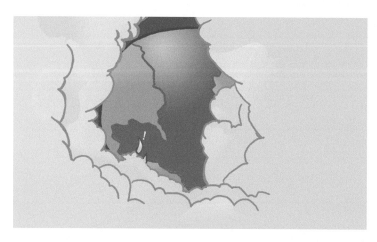

Author

Peter W. Carbone, MBA

(T.A.R.A.)
To Always Reach Above!

Illustrations by
Andrea Montano

Ben the Raindrop's depiction created by
Brionna Carbone

About the book:

Ben The Raindrop is an inspirational character whose focus is to teach children the importance of perseverance, inspiration and leadership. It is an interactive series, which introduces these important characteristics with the use of a creative story, beautiful illustrations and a short question and answer section. In short, Ben The Raindrop will assist children with the important lessons of self-assurance.

<u>Note to the parents, teachers and mentors</u>:

You are about to embark on a very important mission (should you accept this mission), which is to teach a child the importance of perseverance and inspiration. You are about to teach a child the importance of trusting in oneself; you are about to teach them self-assurance.

Even though this is a children's book, you must accept the responsibility that you do have the power and ability to influence a child in a positive fashion. Please do not take this gift for granted.

It is for this reason that I have decided to write this prelude. There are a couple of key words that are within the story that should be defined for the child reading this book. Please take the time to read the definitions (below). Once you define the words, explain, in your words, the meaning of each word. Lastly, ask the child to explain the definition back to you in his/her words. Then begin the story. As you both journey the story and you get to one of the words, ask the child if he/she remembers, generally, the meaning of the words.

At the end of the story, review the words and ask how the execution of the meaning of those words made a difference in Ben the Raindrop's life. This will insure you that the child appreciated the intent of the story. Then review with the child the six questions that are at the end of the story. Lastly, have fun! Enjoy your time. Read with enthusiasm and with purpose. Remember: be great and inspire!

Word definitions:

Dedicated: Set apart for a purpose; committed.

Destiny: That which is to happen in the future.

Effort: A putting forth with strength; use of resources toward a goal.

Effortless: Not putting forth any effort. No attempt to accomplish.

Enthusiasm: Strong excitement of feeling or its cause.

Evaporate: Pass off in or change into vapor. Disappear.

Indomitable spirit: If there is an injustice, one must continue to overcome obstacles no matter how difficult the situation, with the intent of stopping the injustice.

Inspiration: Influence by action; stir into action; bring about.

Obstacles: Something that stands in the way or opposes a person or something.

Passion: Excitement, enthusiasm, zeal

Perseverance: Never stop trying. To continue a course of action no matter how difficult.

Purpose: Intent; Something (as a result) aimed at. A mission.

Self-Control: Control of one's own emotions, desires, or actions.

✖ Definitions found in the Webster's New World Dictionary.

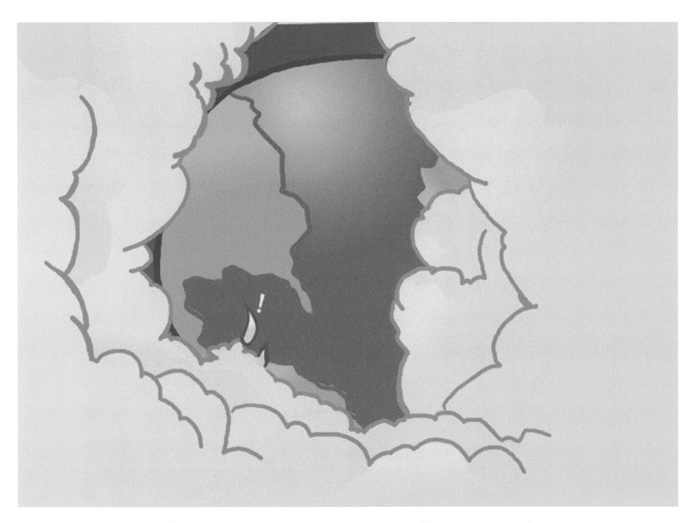

Persevere And You Will Succeed

Upon the time of an incredible rain shower, there were formed two very special raindrops, high up in a cloud. One raindrop was named Ben and the other raindrop was named Clyde.

Ben and Clyde noticed that they were two of many billions and billions of raindrops. Ben looked up, down and all around with incredible enthusiasm and passion. Clyde was somewhat surprised when he heard Ben say how much of a difference he was planning on making with his life and the lives of others. Ben said that he would accomplish this mission while he is striving to realize his true potential.

Clyde looked at Ben and said that he was crazy. "Look at all of us. There are millions, billions and trillions of us raindrops. How do you think you are going to make a difference?"

Ben didn't even hear him. He was just too busy shouting to the world, "Look out below! Here I come!"

Clyde just rolled his eyes and continued to fall <u>effortlessly</u> to earth and said, "Ben, you need to chill, all that <u>passion</u> might cause you to <u>evaporate</u>!" They began to laugh.

"No way," replied Ben, "I plan on making a difference in this world. Clyde, we were formed for a <u>purpose</u>. We have to work hard and fulfill our <u>destinies</u>. We can do that by living up to our potential."

Again Clyde rolled his eyes and said, "Ya! Whatever Ben."

Ben then closed his eyes and thought about what he could do to make a difference in the world. After a short duration of time, he decided that he wanted to bring beauty into this world, but how?

Once Ben opened his eyes he saw a big, beautiful, colorful rainbow arching up toward him. He had never seen anything like it in his short life. He felt he must bring beauty into the world and now he knows one way he can accomplish this goal.

"Come-on Clyde, over there, look at that rainbow!" Ben did all he could do to fall toward the rainbow. With all his might, all the strength in his body and all his will, he decided to work toward his potential and add beauty to the world.

Ben's actions were demonstrating <u>perseverance</u> to succeed; a characteristic that Clyde appeared to lack.

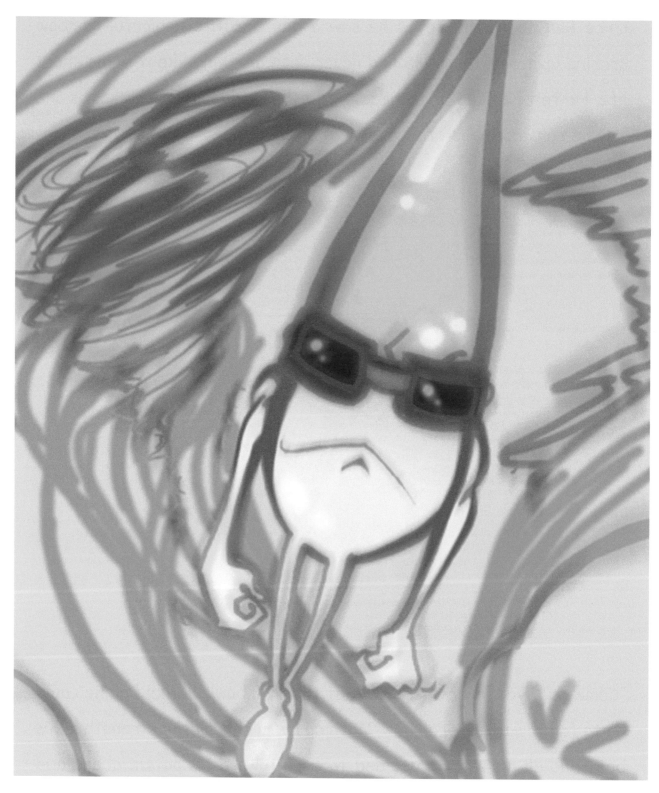

"Come on Clyde!" yelled Ben as he continued to fight the strong winds that were working against him. Ben was trying with much effort to work his way toward the vibrant rainbow. He was overcoming great adversities while developing an <u>indomitable spirit</u>.

"No way, that takes too much effort, I'll meet you below," Clyde responded as he continued to fall effortlessly down towards the earth.

With much work and skillfulness, Ben finally made it to the very top of the rainbow as he continued his journey. As he was absorbed into the first color of the rainbow, he became surprised by the sunlight and the warm, tingling sensation.

At that very moment, his efforts and unwavering dedication to his mission proved victorious; Ben was about to add beauty to the world.

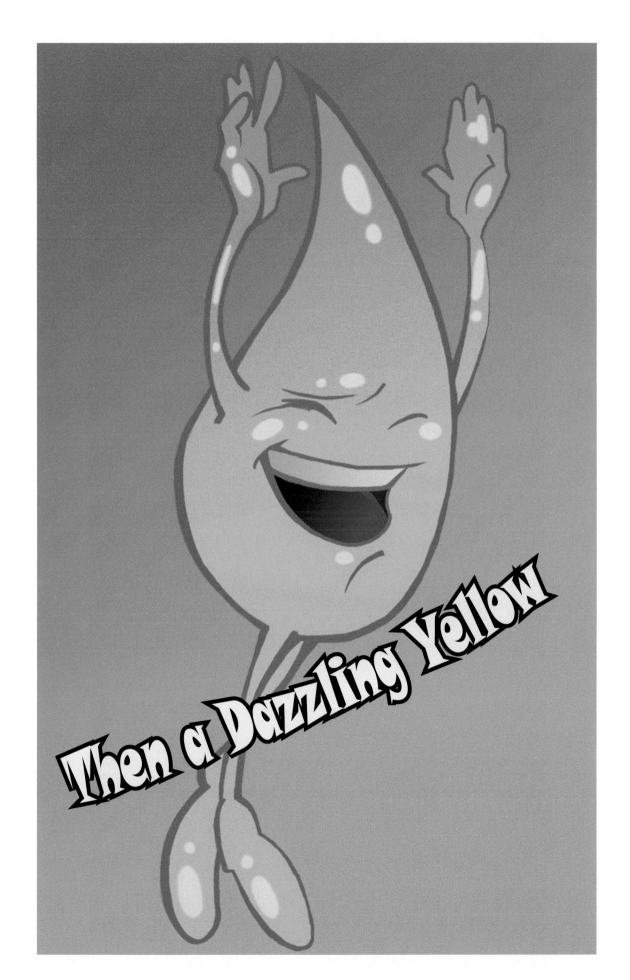

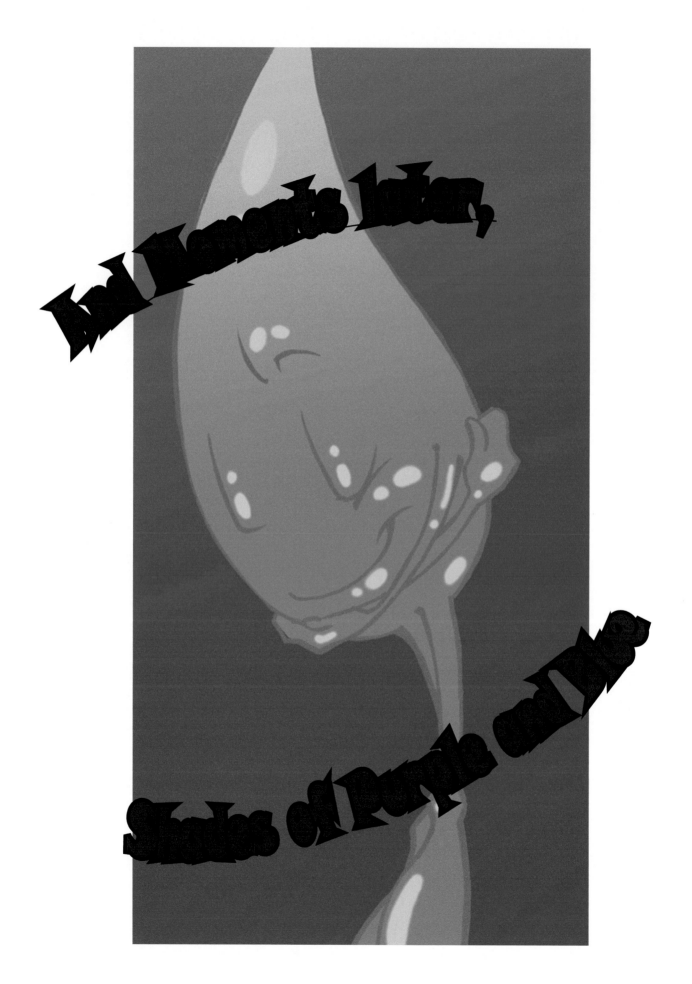

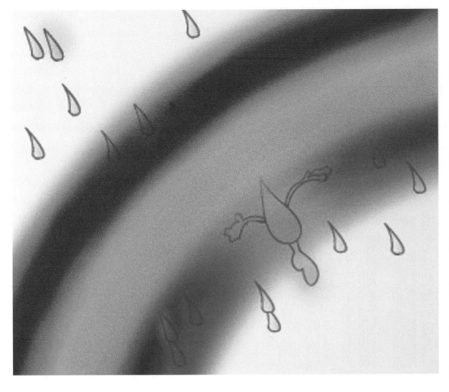

He yelled out, "Look at me world, I am part of a beautiful rainbow!" He could actually see excited, smiling mothers and children on the ground pointing up at him.

Clyde was far away from Ben now, however, he was amazed at what he had seen. "Wow, Ben that was great!"

Ben yelled out to Clyde, "Come with me Clyde, we can make a difference together!" He was very focused on his <u>destiny</u> as he continued with his journey down towards earth.

"I don't know Ben, let me think about it. You are so far away now; it will take a lot of <u>effort</u> on my part to go against the strong jet steam and winds. Falling my way just seems so much easier." Clyde said this as he continued to descend <u>effortlessly</u>.

"Clyde, over here, come on, I know how I am going to add more beauty to this world!" Ben kept calling for his friend, however Clyde could not hear him; they were simply too far apart.

As Ben raced toward the earth to meet his <u>destiny</u>, he spotted colors on the ground that reminded him of the beautiful rainbow through which he had just fallen.

It took a lot of <u>effort</u> but Ben was <u>dedicated</u> because he believed in himself, his mission and his potential. When he found himself tiring from the <u>obstacles</u> the strong wind and the jet stream created, he found himself remembering his mission, **"to strive to reach my potential and add beauty to the world."** This motivated him to fight those winds even harder and struggle toward those charming colors on the ground. He stayed focused on his goal as he worked through his obstacles.

He was finally completely above those lively colors when he noticed the colors were flowers. "Wow," he exclaimed, "I know my <u>destiny</u>. I know how I am going to add beauty to this world."

He aimed straight for the inside of a red rose that had yet to blossom. Like a diver propelling herself off a diving board as she stylishly summersaults and then dives <u>effortlessly</u> and gracefully into the water without a splash, Ben completed his journey by diving straight into the center of the rose.

He knew the rose welcomed him. Just as he sank into the center of the rose, the rose petals began to stretch out her glorious arms and blossom to show all her wondrous and miraculous traits. It is her beauty that will now inspire others.

It was as if the rose was expressing her appreciation to Ben by making the world a more charming place. Nothing could be more beautiful.

Ben's destiny was fulfilled because he believed in himself; he not only had an unwavering faith, but also <u>self-control</u>. He therefore, overcame his <u>obstacles</u> and worked to achieve his <u>purpose</u>.

Clyde, however, was never able to get motivated. He consistently lacked self-control and he lacked the desire to be productive; in short, he was lazy. As a result, he developed poor habits and, consequently, poor health.

What ultimately happened to Clyde? He fell to the pavement and finished his journey in a big muddy puddle.

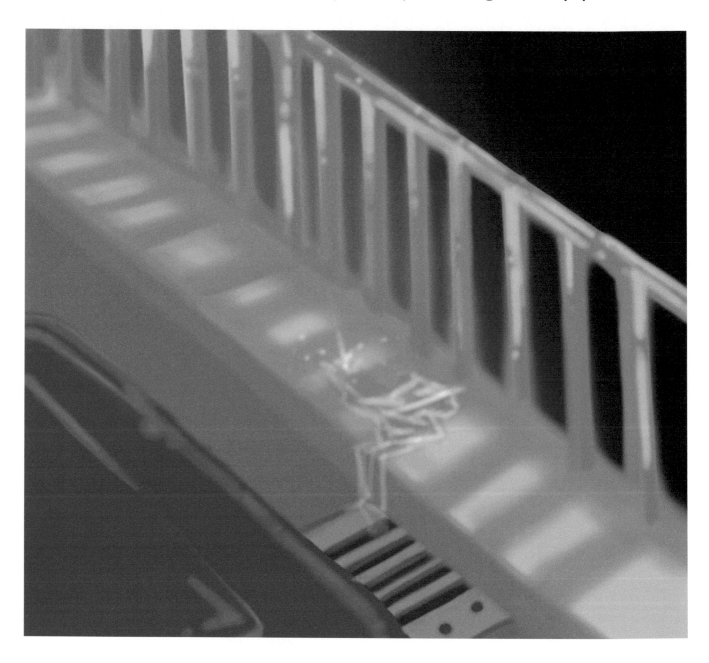

Workbook

Once you and your child have completed the story about Ben the Raindrop, ask the following six questions (below). Have the child answer the questions to you in his/her own words. This will assist the child in better understanding the purpose of Ben's adventure. Finally, explain to the child how he/she can accomplish his/her own goals by believing in their own strength; their strength of believing in themselves just as Ben the Raindrop believed in his own strength.

Questions and Answers

1. What was Ben's inspiration?
   - ❖ Fulfilling his purpose
   - ❖ Touching people's lives

2. According to Ben, what was his destiny?
   - ❖ To add beauty to the world

3. Name at least two of Ben's obstacles?
   - ❖ The strong winds and jet-stream
   - ❖ His friend, Clyde (He was a cynic, a doubter)

4. What is the difference between Ben and Clyde?
   - ❖ Ben was willing to work toward his goal. Ben believed he could make a difference in the world and in his own life. Even though there were billions of other Raindrops, Ben believed in himself. Clyde, on the other hand, was lazy. He just wanted to fall "effortlessly." He did not believe in himself.

5. When Ben found he was tiring from the strong winds (his obstacles) did he just give up and quick trying? What did he find?

   ❖ No, Ben never quit trying. He had faith in himself and he persevered. Ben had an indomitable spirit and continued to fight so he could reach his potential and fulfill his destiny.

   ❖ What he found was a beautiful rainbow that he helped perpetuate. He then found a beautiful rose, which he helped because the rose was in need of water to grow, blossom and therefore be able to inspire others.

6. What happened to Clyde? Why did his journey end this way?

   ❖ He ended his journey in a big muddy puddle.

   ❖ He lacked self-control, an indomitable spirit and he was too lazy to persevere through obstacles. He became unfit and unhealthy, which inevitably will lead him down an unfortunate path.

Give an example of when you kept trying and accomplished your goal. What was the result?

About the Author:

The author, Peter W. Carbone, is also the author of Ben the Raindrop (Strength in Leadership), REACH Presentation Skills, and the RISE (Rare Disease) Selling Framework.

Printed in the United States
by Baker & Taylor Publisher Services